ORCHARD BOOKS
96 Leonard Street, London EC2A 4XD
Orchard Books Australia
32/45-51 Huntley Street, Alexandria, NSW 2015
1 84121 224 5
First published in Great Britain in 2002
Copyright © Adrian Reynolds 2002
The right of Adrian Reynolds to be identified as the author and illustrator
of this work has been asserted by him in accordance
with the Copyright, Designs and Patents Act 1988.
A CIP catalogue record for this book is available from the British Library.
1 3 5 7 9 10 8 6 4 2
Printed in Hong Kong/China

Pete and Polo's Magical Christmas

Adrian Reynolds

ORCHARD BOOKS

To Bronwyn and Ken

Christmas was coming.
Pete was thinking about his Christmas presents.

Pete already knew what
he wanted. He had seen
the best digger ever in
the toyshop window.

Pete asked Polo what present he wanted.
Polo was reading a book from the library
all about polar bears.

"Polar bears love snow," he sniffed, "but I've never
seen any. I'd really like some snow for Christmas, Pete."

Pete remembered seeing snow once, when he was very little, but he didn't know how to make it happen. So he went to ask Mum.

"I know," she said, "why don't we all go and see Santa tomorrow morning? You can ask him about snow."

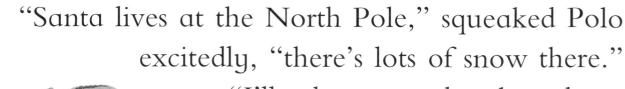

"Santa lives at the North Pole," squeaked Polo
excitedly, "there's lots of snow there."
"I'll take my rucksack and my
wheelbarrow," said Pete, "so
we can bring lots back."

"Good idea," said Polo, "I'll take the bucket and spade."

Next morning, they hadn't driven very far,
when Mum stopped the car.

"I thought we were going to the North Pole!" cried Pete.
"No, silly," Mum laughed, "Santa has come all this way
to the toyshop to see you and all the other children."

For the first time ever, Pete and Polo were disappointed to be at the toyshop, and the queue to see Santa was very, very long.

At last, they got to Santa's grotto.
"Ho, ho, ho!" laughed Santa, "and
what would you like for Christmas?"
Pete asked about the
snow for Polo.

"Hmm," said Santa, "snow can be very tricky. It takes a lot of Christmas magic." Then he whispered, "But you could help make the magic of Christmas stronger."
Pete and Polo moved closer . . .

"The secret of Christmas magic is making other people happy," said Santa.

On the way back home, Pete and Polo thought of what Santa had said.

"How can we make Mum and Gran and Grandpa happy?" asked Polo.

"I know," said Pete, "we could make them some Christmas presents."

As Christmas got closer, Pete and Polo got more excited.
They felt the magic get stronger as they made . . .

a necklace for Mum . . .

a picture for Grandpa . . .

and a jewellery box for Gran.

They almost forgot all about snow . . . almost!

They had only just finished wrapping
the presents on Christmas Eve, when
Gran and Grandpa arrived.

By now, Pete and Polo were feeling very tired.
Gran took them upstairs and read
them a bedtime story.

That night, something magical happened.

The next morning, when they
looked out of the bedroom window,
they couldn't believe their eyes . . .

There was snow everywhere!
More snow than Pete and Polo
could ever have dreamed of!

"Mum," cried
Pete as they rushed
downstairs, "Santa's been,
and he's brought snow for Polo!"
"I know," said Mum, "and I
think he's left something for you, too!"

And there, next to the Christmas
tree, was the best digger
Pete had ever seen.

They all played out in the garden that morning. Gran made a snowman. Mum and Grandpa threw snowballs. Pete and Polo played in the digger.

And they all agreed that this was their best Christmas ever.

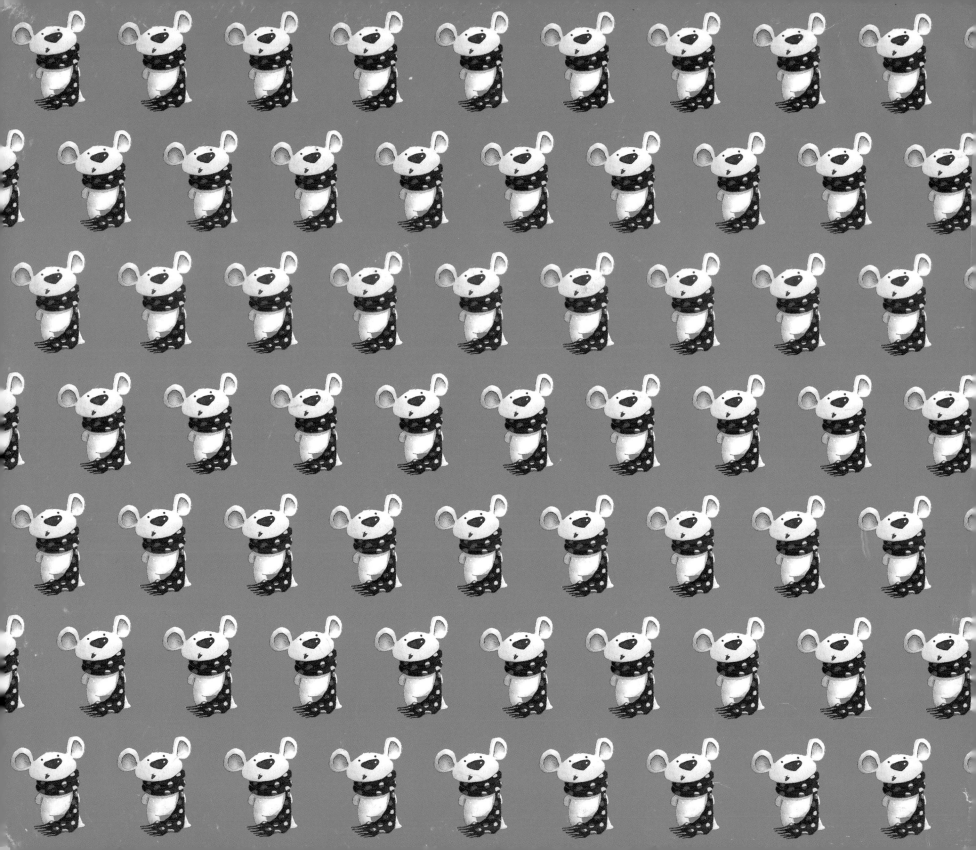